Copyrig

Self- published by
C.E. Metcalf

Hero's From The Grave

By C.E. Metcalf

Everyone needs a hero. There is no strength stronger than love. Even from

the ones that are no longer with us.

Some stories say that hero's never truly die that their souls remain amongst the living to protect the ones they love. Weather that is fact or fiction know one truly knows. But in this case.......

Chapter 1

The last thing I remember I had just returned home after a tour in Afghanistan. I came home to a loving welcome home from both my son and my wife. My son David had just turned twelve and was as tall as me. My wife Cathy the love of my life was expecting our next child within the next month. I was so glad to be home at last. My tour lasted twenty-eight months. If I never see sand again it will be too soon. Cathy prepared a fantastic meal that night it was fit for royalty. Our son David wanted to tell me what went on in his life all in one night. He didn't have school the next day, so we just let him talk until he fell asleep on the couch.

Cathy and I headed for bed. As I was getting undressed, she could see the battle scars on my body. I couldn't help but notice she was starting to cry. Why do you keep putting yourself through this she asked? I fight for the things I

love I said. I love
our country and
most of all I love you
and David.

I know sooner got
the words out of my
mouth and I heard a
noise that made my
skin crawl. Like hell
I said to myself as I
jumped up and
grabbed my pistol

from our night-stand. Our bedroom door open and four masked people came through. I shot one in the forehead dropping the person to the ground. The second attacker tried to kick me in the face and missed as I drove my fist into its kneecap. As the second attacker fell to the floor screaming my chest exploded in pain as a bullet went into my chest killing me.

Two years have gone by since that night. Through the darkness I could hear a faint cry for help and soon realized it was my son. In the coldest of my coffin, I could feel my heart slowly start to beat. One beat and then another my strength was returning. How can this be I'm dead? Or am I.

The next thing I knew I was standing on the ground looking at my grave- stone.

Edward David Steel

1980- 2014

Loving husband and father.

I heard again that cry for help and this

time I asked where are you, David? A force that I had never experienced before was telling me what I had to do. A power greater than myself was pulling me away from my grave. The power of Love. My son needed me, and

I will search through Hell to find him if necessary.

As I walked through the city of New York I caught a glimpse of my reflection in a store window. I couldn't help but notice I looked dam good for a dead man. My clothes were even clean. When I looked at myself closer, I was much younger than my death age. I didn't look much over thirty. I kept hearing a voice in my head telling me to prepare for war. A war worse than anything I have seen before. A war against good and evil whatever that meant. I always knew the difference between the two at least I thought I did. I could feel the force inside me pulling at my soul pulling me away from the store window.

For some reason I had compulsion to run. My legs didn't even feel like my own. I started running faster than I ever did in my life. I jumped over a parked car like I was jumping a mud puddle. I passed a moving taxi like it was sitting still. What have I come back at? At this point I didn't care. Before I knew it, I was standing in front of my old address. The house was dark and run down. The grass in the lawn was knee high. I walked up the five steps to the front porch and listened. I heard nothing. The door had been locked from the outside with a padlock. And a crime scene tape was across the front. The memories of that night were rushing back into my head. And the anger burned in my soul like fire.

I took hold of the padlock and squeezed, and I watched it crumble like dust as it fell to the floor. My hand didn't even have a mark on it. Hoping it was still there I had built a secret room off the bedroom where I kept my military stuff.

I opened the door and stepped inside, and it was like stepping back in time. The downstairs was just like I had left it. Everything was in its place.

Even thou it was covered with dust. The upstairs I knew would be different. Taking one step at a time I headed to the second floor. When I got there, I found our bedroom door wide open, and it looked like hell had broken loose. There was blood everywhere along with things smashed. The one thing that hadn't been moved was our dresser. I slowly moved it off to the side so I could get to the hidden door. At the time I build the room I was hoping I was never going to have to use it. We had even wall papered over the door. Taken my finger- tips I felt for the edges of the door feeling for the hidden button that opened it. When I found it, the door popped open ripping the wallpaper around it. The room I had designed was only six-by-ten feet in size. Hanging on every inch were weapons of every kind. And I was highly trained on every one of them. I had put a small safe in one corner where

I had special documents hidden. I didn't bother turning the combination lock I just grabbed the handle and pulled. When the door broke loose I just through it to one side. Laying inside I had a large envelope with every id I needed. The thought of my son needing me kept going around in my head. How can I help you if I don't know where you are? You know what to do the voice said. And then there was silence.

The silence before the storm.

I strapped a knife holster under each pant leg. And then a pistol holster under the back of my shirt. I then put on a bullet proof vest. Around my waist I put on a belt with two more holsters.

And my belly pack had more than enough rounds for a small war.

I took one last look at my hidden room and shut the door. This will be my last visit to my old home. Home is where the heart is and mine isn't here anymore.

My son's voice called for me again louder each time. I felt like I was being pulled like a magnet to where I didn't have any idea. I stood in the middle of the street facing one way and then another. Just waiting for something or even a sign telling me what to do next. Sometimes the signs are right in front of you, and you don't even see them. So many people overlook the obvious and I don't want to be one of them. Not this time not ever.

Visions of Cathy and David were going through my head. Cathy was crying at the top her lungs while two men were rapping her. Another man had my son David bent over a table and he was about to screw him in the ass, and someone said like hell you will. That voice was mine. I was standing in the same room they were. How I got there I had no idea. Who the fuck are you? Said the man who had my son. Like lightning I had a knife across his throat. I'm the man from hell and that's where you're going as I drew my knife across his neck. Just before he fell to the floor he looked into my eyes, and he knew who I was. You son of a bitch one of the other men screamed. I just held my ground and laughed. All you two are just a couple of pussies? They only way you can get laid is by rapping innocent woman. And you blow buddy here is just a sick bastard that deserved to die.

I of them through a knife at my head and I grabbed it in med air and through it back planting it between his eyes. The last one came at me with his bare hands and said I'm going to kill you mother fucker. I don't think so because I'm already dead. I made my fingers into a point thrusting into his chest. As I held his still beating heart in my hand, I asked him how it feels to get your heart ribbed out. I squeezed every ounce of blood from his heart and through it on the floor beside him.

By this time David had his pants pulled up and was sitting on the floor in a ball. His face showed no emotion and not a sound came from his lips. I knew he was in shock.

Cathy was still lying on the bed with a face full of tears. Her clothes were ripped and there was blood between her legs. I softly took hold her hands and sat he up. We I looked into her eyes she knew who I was. I had just turned thirty when we got married. She couldn't help but remember my eyes. The eyes that love her so. How can this be she asked? I watched you die and get buried. She put her arms around me and squeezed me so hard my eyeballs almost popped out.

I turned my head and David was standing beside me. Not a word came from his lips. I slowly put by arms around him and gave him a hug. Everything will be ok

I promise. I could see the tears forming in his eyes. With a broken voice he asked is it really you dad? Yes, son it is. I don't know how but I know why. Your voice was calling me for help through the darkness and here I am.

But how Dad your dead? Some soldiers never truly die their souls remain here to protect the ones they love. We they are needed they come to help. Why son I really don't know. That's been a story that has been passed down through the centuries. Will you been leaving again asked David? Probably when I know your safe. But no matter where you are I will be watching over you and guarding you from harm. You might say I'm your guardian angel. That's pretty- cool said David. Cathy on the other hand still couldn't believe it.

I stood there and listened for a minute as the sirens were coming. Some how they got the report that something went down here. You will be ok now I promise as my image faded away from their eyes.

Cathy called my name and said thank you, but I didn't answer. I was still there but they couldn't see me. My soul was just there.

I could see the tears in Cathy's eyes as she said I love you. And in a soft voice like a whisper, I said I love you to.

Once the cops and the E M T's showed up, I faded away into nothingness.

I stood one again in front of my grave

looking at my head stone. A mysterious force was pulling me downward. I laughed a little and grinned as I slowly was lowered back into my resting place. As I laid in my coffin, I could feel my heartbeat slow down like a battery that was dying one beat at a time until it stopped. And then there was nothing.

Normally when you die your body rots away in your casket. And all that is left is bone. Most of the time I would agree you but not this time. Somewhere in the world another soldier is rising from his grave. And the cycle continues. Just like it has for hundreds of years. No one ever knows how it happens. Some people won't even admit it even when they saw it happen. Usually, it's the ones that do see them they themselves think they must be going crazy. Then again, some are. I guess we will truly know what fact or fiction is.

Chapter 2

The year is 1967 sergeant Robert O'Conner was found dead in the battlefield. After getting in the back by a Vietnamese snipper. He didn't even know what hit him. The shell hit him in the left of his back and straight through his heart. He was dead before he hit the ground.

After the battle was over a, Army Medic checked his dog tags to see who he was. He took one dog tag and placed it between his teeth. And the other he put in his med bag so he could give it to his commanding officer. That was the protocol when a soldier gets killed in battle. Then his body is placed in a body bag and sent to the nearest medical unit to get cleaned up and sent home for burial. He was one of the lucky ones they even found. Some soldiers were blown to pieces and the medic had all he could do just to find any body parts at all.

Within a few days Sergeant Robert O'Conner's body was

sent back to Middletown Virginia for his service and burial. He left behind a wife Louise and two daughters Becky and Beverly. They were three and four.

He was only twenty-nine when he was

killed, and Louise was twenty-six.

The whole town was at his service. For a young man he was known by a lot of people. I guess small towns can be that way.

For the first year Louise came to visit his grave almost

everyday rain or shine. As time passed those visits became further apart. And for some reason she didn't come anymore. Ten years had come and went and then one rainy night Robert O'Conner started breathing again. At first, he screamed when he realized where he was. And then he started to laugh. And then it happened a mysterious force he had no control over pulled up through the six feet of dirt that was on top of him.

As he looked down
at his empty grave
the thunder echo
the night and the
lighting filled the
sky. And a voice was
crying for help that
knew quite well. It
was Louise. A force
was pulling him
away from his grave
something he had

no control over.
Where he was going,
he had no idea. He
found himself
standing in front of
what looked like a
crack house.
Louise's voice
became louder. It
sounded like a cry
for help. When he
entered the house

there were people shooting up in various places. When he walked through no one even noticed or they just didn't care. Off in a side room he found Louise with a needle handing out of her arm. She was hardly breathing almost dead. He carefully removed the needle. He removed a knife from his pocket and made the needle hole bigger and started sucking the drug from her body like a vampire sucking blood from his victim.

Within seconds her heartbeat start to pick up and get stronger. By now he was holding her in his arms trying to wake her. Slowly one breath and then another she came back to life. When she finally noticed who was holding her, she started to cry. How she asked in between the tears. You called me for help and I'm here Robert said. And help you I will. First, I need to get you out of here and to somewhere safe.

Reaching down he picked her up with

ease and held her like a newborn child in his arms. No one else seemed to care as he carried her down- stairs and out the front door. It was like they didn't even see them. Her weight seemed like a bag of sugar to him.

The nearest hospital was not a mile away. It only took him a few minutes to get there. When he walked in the Emergency Entrance the whole place came to life. One of the aids came running up with a wheelchair. And he gently sat her in it. When the aid turned to look at him, he was gone. He could see the aid, but no one could see him. He was a ghost amongst the living.

He knew that his job was done for now anyway. He walked out of the hospital in silence at least to him it was.

There was a stillness in the night like the stillness of a graveyard. He could see no one on the city streets. There was no movement of any kind. It seemed like the whole city was dead at least it did to him.

That mysterious force was starting to pull him again. This time he didn't try and fight it he just walked along in the direction that it wanted him to go. This time he knew where he was going back to his place of rest until he was needed again.

It took him about a half hour to get back to the cemetery. His grave was just like he had left it. It looked like not even a pebble was out of place. As he stood and looked at his head stone the ground opened like a set of double doors and his casket was open waiting for him to lie in it.

At first, he didn't want to do it. But a feeling of peace came over him as he laid down with ease. As he closed his eyes the lid of the casket closed, and the ground filled itself back in. And a cold silent sleep came over him as his soul finally found peace.

He never again had to come to the rescue of his wife. After a stay in the hospital and a long-term rehab she got clean and made something of herself. She had gotten married again and had three more children. And she was happy.

Every so often she think about the night Robert saved

her. And both a smile and tears were on her face.

Their daughter's Becky and Beverly had both grown up and had families of their own. And they were all one big happy family.

An old man lies in a bed in a vet's home

the year is 1986. He had no family that the staff knew about. Then one day he had a visitor. Another old man about his age came to see him. The man's name was Michael O'Donnell they had served in Vietnam together.

They had not seen each other since the end of the war. The man lying in bed his name was Jacob Maloney. They've been friends since boot camp.

As they talked about old times A tear came to Michael O'Donnell eyes. He

knew that his
friends time on
earth was over. They
had many good
times together.
Jacob looked at
Michael and smiled
and closed his eyes
and peacefully went
to sleep for the last
time. Michael gave
his old friend a kiss

goodbye on his forehead and then sadly left. Knowing in his heart he had lost the best friend he had.

Michael O'Donnell was given a military funeral. There were only three people there. And they were some of the staff of the hospital. Everyone thought he didn't have any family. Or did he?

Ten Years have passed since Michael O'Donnell was laid to rest. Just like the soldiers before him he was waken from his eternal sleep. When he arose from his grave, he too took the form of a younger man. While he stood by his grave in astonishment not knowing what the hell had happened. A voice was crying for help. He to was pulled away from his grave by a strange power that he had no control over. It was a child's voice that he didn't recognize or remember. It felt like he was being pulled like a magnet. To where he had no idea. All he knew was that he had to answer a cry for help. As he walked down the sidewalk, he noticed a young girl was trying to cross the street and a car was heading right for her. In the blink of an eye, he was pulling her away just before the car would have hit her.

He looked at her face and his turned to stone. The face he was looking at was his daughter. She was hit by a drunk driver and killed years before. Or was she?

Can it be that he went back in time to save her from that. But how?

He safely carried her to the other side of the street and placed her back on her feet.

Where the hell did you come from, she asked? I thought

sure I was a goner. It doesn't matter where I came from what matters is that I did.

Are you ok now he asked? Yes, she said I think so. Then he just smiled and said be more careful Cindy. And he started to walk away. How do you know my name she asked? It doesn't matter he said as he disappeared into the shadows.

It was a peaceful night as he walked not knowing exactly why it was, he didn't really care. A feeling of peace had come over him. A feeling you get when deep down in your soul you know you did the right thing.

Just around the corner is the cemetery and his resting place. The gate to the cemetery was locked but he jumped over it with ease. As he walked up to his grave the ground opened and six feet down was his open coffin. He didn't want to lay back in it be he knew he had to.

As he laid down, he could feel a coldness come over him. A coldness you get just before you die. But his was a little different. As he laid his head down for the last time his final words were I love you, Cindy.

Because of that night Cindy's life changed. Instead of dying she was raised by her grandparents, and she made something of her life. Years later she was going through some real old photos that her grandmother had kept. And she ran across a photo of the man that had saved her life. She asked her grandmother who he was. At first, she didn't want to tell her, but she finally did. That photo is your father her grandmother said. Your mother had an Affair with a married man. She didn't know it until after she got pregnant.

She raised you by herself for a while until her drinking took over her life. And that's when you came to live with us. Do you remember you were fourteen? I remember some of it said Cindy. What every happen to my father she asked?

He died in a nursing home at seventy-eight, He had cancer. His name was Michael O'Donnell. I was told that his wife left him when she found out about you. And she took their children with her. That means I have some siblings. Yes, but I have no idea where they are or even if they are still alive said her grandmother. That would be nice to know if they were said Cindy. If I have any brothers or sisters, I would like to meet them. But be prepared you might not like what you find said her grandmother. Maybe someday should Cindy.

Do you know where my father is buried Cindy asked? I'm sorry honey I don't said her grandmother.

That night Cindy had a dream she went to visit her father's grave. But she was a little girl. How old she was not sure. The dream did not make a lot of sense to her because she was told her father died in a nursing home. Or did he?

That is one of those things she will never know. Sometimes life just is what it is.

Chapter 3

Today is Jack Davis birthday he just turned 31 years old. He has been a state trooper for 10 years. He was doing his patrol of Hwy 69 in Omaha Nebraska. When he Received a call over his radio. Harrison bank has been robbed the getaway car was headed in his direction. Other responders are on the way. he then spun his car around sideways blocking the highway. He then quickly grabbed a rifle from his trunk. The left side of his car was facing Outward. As he stood on the other side, he placed his rifle under roof and waited. He could hear the roar of a speeding car coming towards him. When he finally spotted it, he took aim. He knew the driver saw him but didn't slow down. He drove the get away car into the side of Jack Davis's police cruiser pushing it over him and killing him.

When the responders finally arrived, they knew it was too late. When they found Jack Davis, his car was on top of him. And they knew he was dead.

There was an extensive line of cars at his funeral. It seemed like he had friends and family from all over that came. Many a tear were shed that day. His parents had lost their only son. That a week went by, and the state had a highway marker put up in memory of him. They put it right in the spot where he was killed. It was bad enough he had died but the bank robbers were never caught. The get away car found in a near by river a year later. The robbers sank it when the tide was high. That would by them some time to get away.

Many years have passed his parents are now elderly. They are still living at their home but barely making ends meet. Their credit has been exhausted. Every day they come that much closer to losing their home. The bank had started their foreclosure. Each morning they would pray together and ask God for help.

That night there was a bad storm the

lighting cracked, and the thunder echoed through the sky. The two of them sat on their front porch is dismay. They watched a bolt of lighting hit something in the distance. Out of the shadows they saw a person walking towards them. As they watched the persons walk seemed so familiar. When the person got close enough, they both couldn't believe their eyes. It was their son Jack. O my God said his father. His mother got up from her chair and slowly walked towards him. How can this be she said between the tears? We watched you get buried, your dead. She reached out and touched his hand and it was cold as ice. It scared her so much she jumped back in fear. Don't worry mom Jack said. I'm here to help you not hurt you. She could no longer hold back she put her arms around him and cried even more. By this time, his father was standing next to him and put his hand on his shoulder. My son he said trying not to cry himself. God has answered our prayer and brought you back to us. Only as a messenger Jack said just to give you this. Out of nowhere Jack handed his father a briefcase. I need to go now everything you need is in here open it when you get inside.

It was late into the night when his parents woke up. They had both falling asleep on the porch like they had many times before. But this night was different on the floor between them laid a briefcase. They both looked at each other and said at the same time it wasn't a dream.

They got up and took the briefcase inside and laid it on their kitchen table. When they opened it, they found piles of cash and receipts for all their bills stating they were paid in full. And the mortgage to the house was free and clear. To this day they believe it was a miracle from God. If you believe in miracles.

Chapter 4

John Sullivan had been a fireman in Brooklyn for over twenty years. He had just turned fifty and was getting close to retiring. He was on the night shift midnight to seven am. Or until he was relieved whatever came first.

It was a cold winter night in November, and he just started his shift when the fire alarm went off. Everyone suited up as fast as they could and got the trucks rolling. The sirens where loud in the quite of the night. One advantage about rolling this late at night the traffic was a lot easier to get through. The address was 552 Hawkins Boulevard. He knew already it was a large apartment building. The place was a shithole because the landlord was a cheap scumbag that didn't want to fix anything. People lived there because they couldn't get a place anywhere else.

As the trucks pulled up, he could see the whole top floor was ablaze. People were running from the building like rats leaving a sinking ship. Within minutes the hoses were hooked up and water was blasting through the air. It was a five- story building but on the fourth floor there was a woman sticking her head out the window screaming for help. The ladder truck hadn't arrived yet, so he had no choice but to go in after her. Four stories up that meet racing up eight flights of stairs and trying to find her.

Two other firemen had already knocked the front door down. The place was some dam old he knew it didn't have a working elevator. At least he didn't think so. He had already put on his oxygen tank and mask and was ready to go. The tank alone weighted forty pounds plus his weight of two hundred.

The first two flighted were easy. By the time he reached the fourth floor he was out of breath. He could hear the woman screaming put through the smoke he couldn't see her yet. When he finally found her, she was lying on the floor by the windowing. The was filled with smoke so think it was worse than fog. He went to pick her up and the ceiling was starting to come down. He took a quick look out the window to see if they had the trampoline in place. When it picked her up he said your not going to like this as he dropped her out the window. He went to jump himself, but the ceiling came down on top of him and he was pinned against the floor. As he laid there only one thought was in his mind his wife Betsey. They were married right out of high school. She was the love of his life. And he knew he was never going to see her again. Both of his arms were pinned by a couple of large beams so he couldn't get to his radio. He could hear his captain calling him, but he couldn't respond.

He could feel his oxygen running out. That meant only one thing he had burst an oxygen when he fell. Normally his tank would last a couple of hours and it hadn't been half an hour yet. His lungs were starting to burn because of the smoke he knew soon he would be unconscious. As his oxygen ran out his life came to an end.

By now the building was ablaze inside and out. Flames were shooting high into the night. Floor after floor the inside of the building was crumbing to the ground. Some of the other fire fighters hung their heads because they knew that John Sullivan didn't make it out.

The word had already gotten to his wife Betsey. Betsey was blind and had been since she was

born. But John
never cared he loved
her anyway. He
thought she was the
most beautiful
woman on earth.
The police chief
himself came to
their home and told
her what had
happened. He could
see the sadness

come over her face as he told her. He followed her into the living room as she sat down in the nearest chair. At first, she was in shock because she couldn't believe her ears. And then it hit her light a rock. She couldn't help but hang her head down and cry. My poor John she repeated. He loved me so much. I don't know what I'm going to do without him.

It took almost a week to make his funeral arrangements. His body was never found because he was burned to ashes. Ashes to ashes dust to dust he shall return. Betsey had no family close, but she had a lot of friends. They all took turns staying with her until after John's funeral. Then she planned on flying to Texas to live with her sister Sandra.

At his funeral a long parade of fire trucks from all over the state came to say goodbye to their brother. His parents were given the key to the city. And a plaque was hung in the fire hall so everyone could see. That afternoon everyone went home to wherever their homes were. Others went to their favorite bar and tried to drink away their sadness. His parents that's another story. Every hate losing a child especially their only one. Their lives were never the same after that day because their never had any closure. They knew their son was dead, but they couldn't except it. There wasn't a day that went by that one or the other of them didn't cry. Why God why they asked may times. They felt they deserved an answer. If only they could then maybe they could finally put his soul to rest.

They were sitting at their kitchen one night and the wind

started to howl like never before. They were both looking out the window watching. For what they didn't know. As they looked close to the ground a dust storm arose it spun like a tiny tornado at first. Inch by inch it grew taller until it reached almost six feet. Out of the wind dirt and dust a figure stepped out. Their son John Sullivan.

The old couple couldn't believe their eyes. Because of their age neither of them could hardly walk. His father was using a cane, and his mother a walker. But they managed to open the front door and go outside. Not a sound was mad from any of them until their son John spoke. I just wanted to tell you everything is the way it's supposed to be. And I'll be waiting for you, and I love you both.

That night his parents kissed each other good night for the last time. One of the neighbors came over for a visit the next morning and found them both. They had died

peacefully in their sleep.

Gomer was a German shepherd he weight around 100 pounds. He belonged to the McKendrick family. Joe and Ann had five boys Chris John Tim Butch and Pat. Gomer was the neighborhood mascot he would wonder around the neighborhood like he owned everyplace. Nobody really cared back then he didn't really bother anyone he would just go to different places to say hello.

That dumb dog had been hit by everything on wheels. A tractor ran over him and it didn't even hurt him. He just rolled over a couple of times and got back on his feet and went back to chasing it.

He was hit my a milk truck one morning it got him with the front bumper, and he went flying into the ditch. He just laid there for a minute stunned and got back on his feet and shook himself off.

One of the local's hit him a station wagon on his way to work and the asshole didn't even stop. He looked in his rearview mirror and noticed Gomer was alright and kept going.

And finally, some passer by hit him in

the head with the front bumper of a V W bug and broke his neck. The whole neighborhood was sad about it, but everyone knew it was an accident. The family buried him in the corner of the back yard. They even made a stone

for him, and it read
Man's best friend
and his name was
placed under that.

A couple of years
had passed, and it
was an ordinary
winter. There was a
pond that all the
neighborhoods
would go skating on.

There was only one rule no one goes there alone. One night Pat the youngest of the five boys couldn't sleep and he went there by himself. He knew he wasn't supposed to be there alone, but he did it anyway. At first, he was having a lot of fun, but he soon realized it was too dark to skate. The thought know sooner left his mind and the ice broke and under he went. He could hardly breath the water was so cold. The shock alone almost killed him.

He wanted to pull himself out, but he couldn't find the hole in the ice that he fell through. He was starting to panic he knew he was going to drown. Then a miracle happened someone was pulling was pulling him up. But the was no hole to go through. When his was just about to bring his head above water he couldn't believe what he saw it was Gomer. He had pulled him out with his teeth. This can't be real Pat said to himself. Gomer brushed up against him just like he used to do. So, Pat reached down and scratched his head. Pat blinked his eyes for only a second and Gomer was gone.

Hero's come in all shapes and sizes. You never know who yours might.

C.E. Metcalf

Made in the USA
Columbia, SC
17 October 2023

24200521R00089